Rockets

MOTLEY'S CREW

Kevin and the Pirate Test

Margaret Ryan &
Margaret Chamberlain

A & C Black • London

Rockets series:

CROOK CATCHERS - Karen Wallace & Judy Brown
MOTLEY'S CREW - Margaret Ryan & Margaret Chamberlain
MR CROC - Frank Rodgers
MRS MAGIC - Wendy Smith
MY FUNNY FAMILY - Colin West
ROVER - Chris Powling & Scoular Anderson
SILLY SAUSAGE - Michaela Morgan & Dee Shulman
WIZARD'S BOY - Scoular Anderson

First paperback edition 2001
First published 2001 in hardback by
A & C Black (Publishers) Ltd
35 Bedford Row, London WC1R 4JH

ISBN 0-7136-5459-7

A CIP catalogue record for this book is available from the British Library.

Printed and bound by G. Z. Printek, Bilbao, Spain.

Chapter One

Kevin, the cabin boy on board the *Hesmeralda,* was lying in his hammock, reading his *Pirate Pete* comics.

Pirate Pete's very brave. I wish I could be more like him...
...but I'm scared of spiders and things that go bump in the night.
I like being a pirate, though. That makes me very happy.

Kevin wasn't quite so happy when Squawk, the ship's parrot, landed on his chest and pecked him on the nose.

READ THIS NOTICE AND YOU'LL SEE
YOU MUST PASS YOUR G.P.S.E.
G.P.S.E? What's that? What are you talking about, Squawk?

Then Kevin read the notice...

'Oh no!' cried Kevin. 'I'm not any good at exams. I get muddled and get things wrong.'

'So I did,' said Kevin and wailed louder than ever.

Captain Motley, Doris McNorris the cook, and Smudger, the first mate, heard the wail.
WAIL
WAIL
He's read the notice.
He's upset.

WAIL BOO HOO
WAIL BOO HOO
SMUDGER
We must help him pass his exam. Let's put our heads together and have a think.

They put their heads together...

'Got it!' said the Captain. 'We know Kevin gets muddled and gets things wrong, so here's what we'll do.'

By the time they found Kevin he was so worried about the exam he had nibbled all ten fingernails and was starting on his toes.

Don't worry about the exam, Kevin. I'll teach you how to moor the ship.
Don't worry about the exam, Kevin. I'll teach you how to mend the sails.
Don't worry about the exam Kevin. I'll teach you how to make pirate porridge.

Squawk looked at the dent in the ship's side where Captain Motley always bumped into the harbour wall. He looked at Smudger's sails still full of holes, and he looked at Doris's apron still covered in last week's lumpy porridge.

'I would worry, Kevin,' he said, and offered him a claw to nibble.

Chapter Two

But Kevin was determined to do his best. He went down to the galley with Doris to learn how to make pirate porridge.

Doris said the first pot was no good.

Doris said the second pot was no good either.

Doris said the third pot was perfect.

Kevin went up on deck to see Smudger to learn how to mend sails.

Smudger said the first sail was no good.

Smudger said the second sail was no good either.

Smudger said the third sail was perfect.

Kevin went to see Captain Motley at the ship's wheel to learn how to moor the ship.

Captain Motley said the first try was no good.

Captain Motley said the second try was no good either.

But Captain Motley said the third time he moored the ship was perfect.

Kevin beamed and puffed out his chest. Not that it made any difference, it wasn't a very big chest.

But someone with a very, very, big chest and a big spyglass had been watching Kevin work hard for his exam.

And Horatio Thunderguts, captain of the *Saucy Stew*, and arch-enemy of Captain Motley, folded up his spyglass and had a think.

His crew could tell he was thinking because his hat popped up and down on his head, his eyes rolled round in their sockets and steam came out of his ears.

After a few minutes Thunderguts stopped popping and rolling and steaming.

But someone else had been keeping an eye on Thunderguts...

And Squawk flew back to the *Hesmeralda* to report to Captain Motley.

‘A cunning plan, you say, Squawk,’ smiled the Captain. ‘Well, good thing we carried out my plan first – let’s see which one wins.’

‘Show off,’ said the Captain.

Chapter Three

The day of the G.P.S.E. arrived. Kevin was so nervous he put his T-shirt on back to front, his trousers on inside out, and stuck his breakfast porridge in his ear.

But it wasn't.

The exam was held on board the Chief Pirate's ship, the *Spic 'n' Span*.

'Bet my porridge is better than yours,' said Dork, the cabin boy from the *Saucy Stew*, who looked different somehow.

The porridge making began. Kevin tried to remember what Doris had told him about making it thick and lumpy, but he was so nervous it came out thin and smooth.

Dork did nothing.

Dork went into his bag and brought out a pot of porridge.

Next was the sail mending.
Kevin tried to remember what Smudger had told him about making the stitches big and dirty, but he was so nervous they came out small and clean.

Dork did nothing.

Dork went into his bag and brought out a sail.

Finally there was mooring the ship.

This ship is my pride and joy
Be careful how you moor her.
CHIEF
If I can sail the Saucy Stew, I can sail this old tub!
Wait a minute! I knew there was something different about you– You're not the cabin boy from the Saucy Stew. You're Captain Horatio Thunderguts in disguise!

NOW WHAT'S KEVIN GOING TO DO ?
HE FACES THE CAPTAIN OF THE SAUCY STEW.
WILL HIS COURAGE FAIL AND GO THROUGH THE FLOOR ?
FIND OUT WHAT HAPPENS IN CHAPTER FOUR !

Chapter Four

All of a sudden Kevin was angry. He was angry about the porridge cheating. He was angry about the sail cheating. And he could feel the anger bubbling in his tum and coming all the way up to his tongue.

And Kevin was so angry he said what Pirate Pete would have said. He said, 'Yes!'

But first he had to moor the ship.
And this time he was so busy thinking about Thunderguts that he forgot all about what Captain Motley had told him and moored it perfectly.

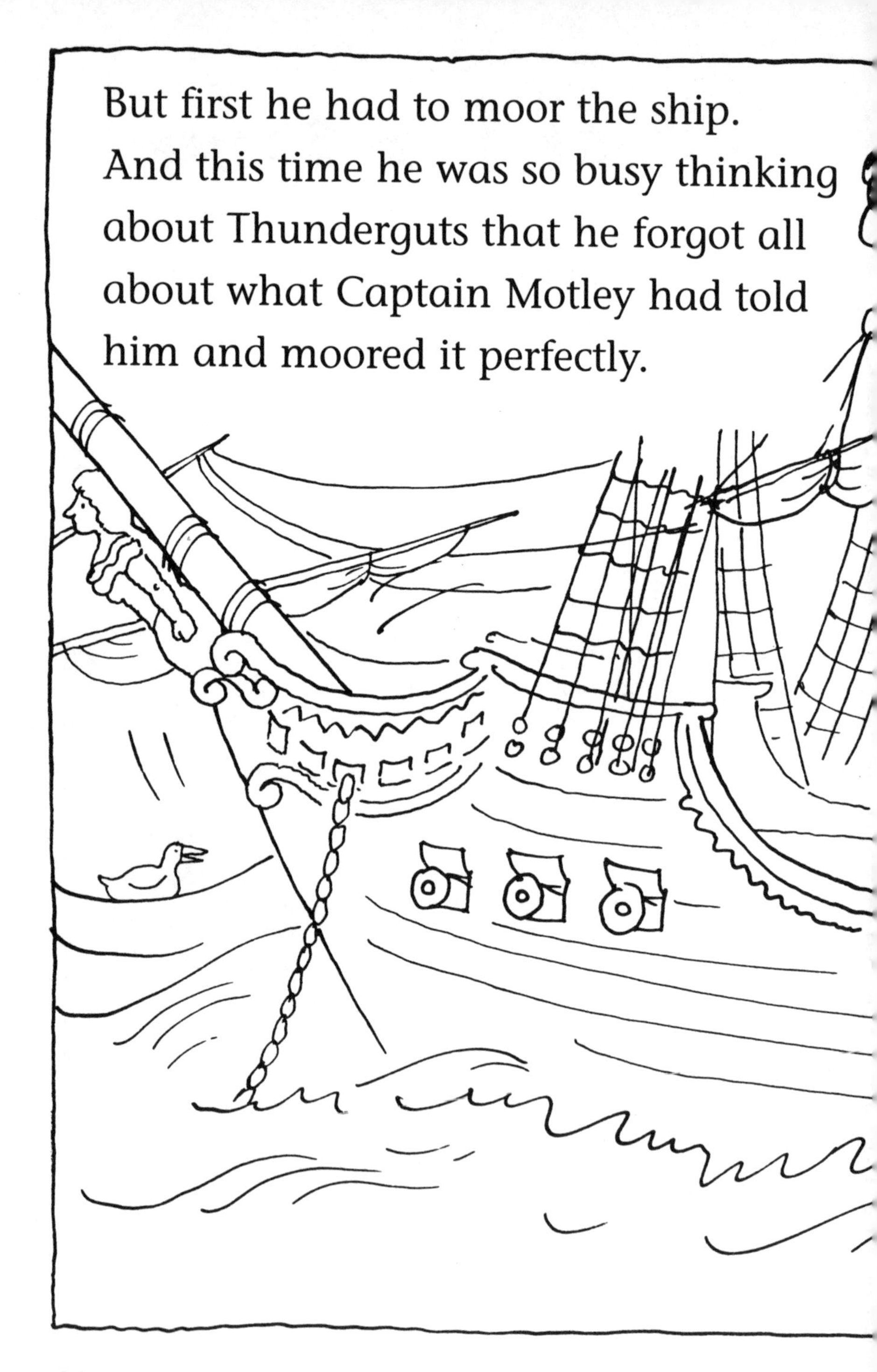

Splendid, splendid. I am happy to tell you, Kevin, that you have passed your G. P. S. E.
Oh but... I thought I did everything wrong... I mean... thankyou very much.

'However,' went on the Chief Pirate, 'I am not happy with one of the other so-called cabin boys who thought he could fool me by cheating.'

'Cheating? Cheating? Oh how awful,' said Horatio Thunderguts, looking round. 'Now who would do a thing like that?'

‘We certainly will go inside,’ said the Chief Pirate. ‘Down to the galley. And you, Thunderguts, will make perfect pirate porridge. If you can do it once you can do it again.’

But Thunderguts couldn’t make the porridge, no matter how often he tried, so the Chief Pirate made him eat all his mistakes.

Then he made him mend all the sails in the entire pirate fleet, but he wouldn't let him moor the *Spic 'n' Span*.

Back on the *Hesmeralda*, Kevin was puzzled.

'I see,' said Kevin, who didn't really.

Or that you really can mend sails that are clean and neat, Smudger?
Er... not really.
What about mooring the ship without making a hole in the side, Captain?
I've always found that a bit tricky.
So have any of you passed your Good Pirate Skills exam, then?
Er, not really.
Not exactly.
Not at all, in fact.

I PASSED MY G.P.S.E!
That was the Good Parrot Squawking Exam, Featherbrain!
That doesn't count.

This is to Certify that Kevin has passed his G.P.S.E
So I'm the only one? Right then, I shall begin teaching you all how to pass your G.P.S.E. tomorrow ...
... after I've read all my *Pirate Pete* comics ... lots of times.